A Tale of Two Cities

Artist: Romano Felmang

First edition for North America (including Canada and Mexico), Philippine Islands, and Puerto Rico published in 2008 by Barron's Educational Series, Inc.

All inquiries should be addressed to:
Barron's Educational Series, Inc.
250 Wireless Boulevard
Hauppauge, New York 11788
www.barronseduc.com

ISBN-13 (Hardcover): 978-0-7641-6138-4
ISBN-10 (Hardcover): 0-7641-6138-5
ISBN-13 (Paperback): 978-0-7641-4007-5
ISBN-10 (Paperback): 0-7641-4007-8

Library of Congress Control No.: 2007906901

Picture credits:
p. 40 Mary Evans Picture Library
p. 43 Topham Picturepoint / TopFoto.co.uk
p. 45 Topham Picturepoint / TopFoto.co.uk
Every effort has been made to trace copyright holders. The Salariya Book Company apologizes for any omissions and would be pleased, in such cases, to add an acknowledgment in future editions.

Printed and bound in China
9 8 7 6 5 4 3 2 1

A Tale of Two Cities

Charles Dickens

ILLUSTRATED BY
Romano Felmang

BARRON'S

RETOLD BY
Jacqueline Morley

SERIES CREATED AND DESIGNED BY
David Salariya

It was the best of times, it was the worst of times, it was the age of wisdom, it was the age of foolishness, it was the epoch of belief, it was the epoch of incredulity, it was the season of Light, it was the season of Darkness, it was the spring of hope, it was the winter of despair…

Charles Dickens, *A Tale of Two Cities*

CHARACTERS

Charles Evrémonde, known as Darnay, a French aristocrat living in England

Sydney Carton, an English lawyer

The Marquis d'Evrémonde, Charles Darnay's uncle

Lucie Manette, a young Frenchwoman living in England

Dr. Alexandre Manette, Lucie's father

Miss Pross, Lucie's companion

Jarvis Lorry, an employee of Tellson's Bank

Jerry Cruncher, a messenger for Tellson's Bank

Mr. Stryver, an English lawyer

Ernest Defarge, a Parisian wine shop owner

Thérèse Defarge, his wife

John Barsad, an English spy

"RECALLED TO LIFE"

1775: a foul November night.

The road from London to Dover.[1]

Exhausted horses are straining to get the mail coach to the top of a hill. Its miserable passengers trudge behind in the mud. They have gotten out to lighten the load.

The passengers are frightened. They know it's dangerous to slow down like this. It makes them easy prey for highwaymen.

Ho there! Stand! I shall fire!

As they climb in again at the top of the hill, they hear a horse galloping behind them. They freeze with terror; the coach guard raises his blunderbuss.[2]

Who wants me? Is it Jerry?

Looming out of the mist, the rider halts and calls to them. Is there a Mr. Jarvis Lorry on board? There is a message for him. It's plainly an urgent one, for the man has ridden hard and is covered with mud.

"Wait at Dover for Mam'selle."[3]

Say that my answer is RECALLED TO LIFE.

"Recalled to life." That's a blazing strange message.

The passenger called Lorry calms the guard. He knows the horseman—he is from Tellson's Bank where Mr. Lorry works. He holds the message under the coach lamp to read it. His reply to the message is a strange one.

As the coach trundles away, the horseman—Jerry Cruncher, official messenger to Tellson's Bank—takes Mr. Lorry's answer back to London. He's puzzled. Whatever can it mean?

1. Dover: a seaport on the south coast of England, used especially by ships sailing to Calais in France.
2. blunderbuss: a shotgun with a short, wide barrel.
3. Mam'selle: short for "Mademoiselle," French for "Miss."

BREAKING THE NEWS

The coach jolts, rattles, and bumps its way through the night, rolling its sleeping passengers about. Mr. Lorry dreams uneasily: he imagines he is in some dark underground place with a key and a candle in his hands, on his way to dig someone out of a grave.

In his dream he is repeatedly questioning a ghostly, haggard face. Question and answer are always the same.

He plies the weary ghost with more questions: "Shall I show her to you?" "Will you come and see her?" The phantom looks despairing and uncomprehending.

He dreams he is digging with the key, or sometimes with a spade or with his bare hands, but the apparition turns to dust as he drags it from the ground.

He starts awake and lets down the carriage window to feel the mist on his cheeks, but out of the night shadows the same ghostly face appears again.

Daybreak at last! From the coach, Lorry gazes with relief and thankfulness at the quiet landscape, the clear sky, and the smiling sun.

1. recalled to life: brought back to life again.

I will relate a story to you, miss, the story of one of my customers.

Later that morning, at an inn in Dover.

Mr. Lorry has come to Dover to meet a young Frenchwoman, Miss Lucie Manette. She is a ward of the bank[1] and, being only 17, is still in its care. He is to accompany her to Tellson's Paris branch because of certain matters which he will explain to her.

Lorry seems unsure how to begin. He is a businessman, used to banking work, not delicate personal matters.

But this is my father's story, sir!

It was you who brought me to England then. I am almost sure it was you.

In heaven's name, why should you kneel to me?

For the truth.

"There was a French doctor who married an English lady. I looked after their affairs in Paris some twenty years ago."

"Their little daughter became an orphan when her mother died, two years after her father."

"But just suppose the girl's father had not died—suppose he had been spirited away by powerful enemies. Suppose the girl's mother, broken-hearted, had only pretended he was dead…"

I am going to see his ghost! It will be his ghost, not him.

Couldn't you tell her what you had to tell her without frightening her to death?

Lorry breaks the news: Lucie's father is alive! He is greatly changed, almost a wreck, but there is still hope for him.

He warns of dangers[2]— her father must not stay in France. But Lucie has fainted, overwhelmed by the news.

Lorry shouts for help and servants immediately rush in. Miss Pross, Lucie's hot-tempered but devoted companion,[3] puts a brawny hand on Lorry's chest and sends him flying.

1. She is a ward of the bank: the bank looks after her money and business affairs, because according to the law she is not old enough to look after herself.
2. dangers: there is political unrest in France, which will lead to the French Revolution of 1789.
3. companion: a person who is paid to look after Lucie and keep her company.

THE SHOEMAKER

Later, in Paris…

How goes it, Jacques?

In the working-class district of St. Antoine, a wine shop stands at the corner of a row of wretched houses. The people are ragged and downtrodden. Yet in the eyes of some there is the gleam of a beast at bay.[1]

The owner of the wine shop, Ernest Defarge, is in close talk with three hungry-looking men whose eyes have that gleam. All of them seem to be called Jacques.[2] Behind the counter Mme.[3] Defarge sits and knits—and listens carefully.

He is greatly changed?

Changed!

A raising of Mme. Defarge's eyebrows warns her husband of the presence of strangers in the shop: an Englishman and a French lady.

Defarge kisses Lucie's hand when he learns that she is the daughter of his former master.

He leads them across a yard and up many stairs. Unlocking a room at the top, he explains that the doctor has been so long imprisoned that he might rave or harm himself if his door were left open.

You are still hard at work, I see.

You can bear a little more light?

I must bear it, if you let it in.

At first they can see nothing in the darkened room. Then they make out a white-haired man with his back to them, busy making shoes.

Defarge speaks firmly and loudly, but he is barely able to attract the man's attention.

The voice that replies is pitiful in its faintness: "Yes—I am working." Then the bent figure lapses into silence and returns to his shoemaking. Defarge opens the shutters wider.

1. at bay: cornered and preparing to fight.
2. Jacques: a code name used by the revolutionaries. Jacques (French for James) was considered a typical name for a peasant, and a peasant rebellion in the 14th century was known as the Jacquerie.
3. Mme.: abbreviation of Madame, the French word for "Mrs."

Mr. Lorry, who has been keeping close to Lucie to reassure her, steps forward softly. Defarge tells the shoemaker that he has a visitor, and asks him to tell Lorry his name.

At first there is no answer. Then, as if from far away, the old man makes a strange reply.

He remembers no other name. Pity overcomes Lucie's fear and she embraces her father. He looks at her in wonder.

He unfolds a scrap of rag that he wears on a string around his neck. It contains a few fine golden hairs—just like Lucie's.

This treasured hair is his wife's. Confused, he wonders if she has come back to him.

Lucie will tell him the truth later, but he must be brought to England at once. While the others organize departure, she stays with him in the locked room, lying beside him in the dark, on the bare floor.

Dr. Manette is guided down to the coach. He has no idea where he is or where he is going. He is just about to enter the coach when he remembers his shoemaking tools. He has left them in the attic.

Mme. Defarge brings the tools down and hands them to him. As the coach drives off she sits by the door, knitting and apparently seeing nothing.

1. gaoler's: jailer's.

TRIED FOR TREASON

Tellson's head clerk calls Jerry Cruncher one day and tells him to hand in a note at the Old Bailey[1] for Mr. Lorry, who is giving evidence at a trial.

When Jerry learns it is a case of treason, he feels a horrid thrill. He knows the penalty—a hideous one.

Jerry gets the note to Mr. Lorry, who is sitting next to the lawyer Mr. Stryver. Opposite them sits a lazy-looking lawyer who stares at the ceiling the whole time.

The prisoner, Charles Darnay, is put in the dock. Everyone, except for the lawyer looking at the ceiling, stares at him. He is about 25, good-looking, plainly dressed, and calm in manner.

The prisoner's face alters as he notices two people to his left: a young woman and a man who is clearly her father. The father's brooding expression makes him look old, but whenever his daughter speaks to him his face brightens and he seems years younger.

The Attorney General claims that Darnay, who travels regularly between England and France, is a traitor passing British secrets to France and America.[3]

Mr. Lorry states that five years ago, when he was returning from France with a lady and gentleman, Darnay travelled on the same boat.

The next witness is Lucie Manette. She confirms that she and her father were travelling with Mr. Lorry that night.

1. Old Bailey: the main criminal court in London, then and now.
2. quartering: men convicted of treason (crime against the state) were "hung, drawn, and quartered." They were hanged until almost dead, then disembowelled and cut into pieces. This punishment was last used in England in 1782.
3. France and America: Britain and France were often at war in the 18th century. Britain was at war with its American colonies (which became the United States) from 1775 to 1781.

Lucie, asked to repeat her conversation with Darnay, is distressed. Darnay was kind to her, and she doesn't want to cause trouble for him.

She is forced to admit that Darnay had told her he was travelling on business that might get people into trouble.

Asked if Darnay was alone, Lucie says that two Frenchmen came on board with him but left before the boat sailed.

Did Darnay speak of the war with America? She says he did—but only to help her understand what the quarrel was about.

The next witness, John Barsad, says he found secret lists in Darnay's desk and saw him snooping around near a dockyard.[1]

Is Barsad sure he saw Darnay with these lists? Certain. Does he hope to gain anything by this evidence? No. He's not being paid to trap Darnay? Oh dear no.

Is he quite sure that the person he saw near the docks was Charles Darnay?

1. snooping around near a dockyard: arson (lighting fires) in a royal dockyard was punishable by death until 1971.

THE LIKENESS

You say that you are sure it was the prisoner. Did you ever see anyone very like him?

Mr. Stryver tries in vain to shake this witness. At this point the lazy-looking lawyer who has been looking at the ceiling all this time scribbles a few words on a piece of paper, crumples it up, and gives it to Stryver.

Stryver unfolds the note, looks very hard at Charles Darnay, and then smiles broadly to himself. He questions Barsad again.

Not so like that I could be mistaken.

Not guilty, my lord.

He asks Mr. Sydney Carton to step forward. The lazy-looking lawyer stands beside Darnay. They are amazingly alike! When Carton removes his wig the likeness is uncanny. He could easily be mistaken for Darnay. Barsad's evidence is discredited—no one can be sure that it was Darnay he saw by the docks.

The jury retires. Carton sees that Lucie's fears for Darnay have made her faint, and he calls for help. The jury returns—and her fears are over.

I am a disappointed drudge,[1] Sir. I care for no man on earth, and no man on earth cares for me.

Much to be regretted. You might have used your talents better.

As Lucie and her father congratulate Darnay, Mr. Lorry sees a strange look pass over Dr. Manette's face—a fleeting expression of mistrust, almost of fear. Lucie takes her father's hand and suggests they go home.

That evening Carton and Darnay dine together. Carton is slightly drunk. It is clear that both men admire Lucie. Carton realizes she has a strong feeling for Darnay; this makes him aware of how different he and Darnay are.

1. drudge: a person who can work hard but has no imagination or enthusiasm.

Darnay says farewell, leaving Carton to fall asleep at the table. He wakes at ten at night and goes to Stryver's chambers.[1] Stryver shows no surprise at finding him the worse for drink.

Carton, with a wet towel around his head, starts work on the next day's cases. This happens every night: Carton does the brainwork and Stryver gets the credit.

At school, Carton did exercises for other boys and seldom did his own. It was the same when he and Stryver were students in Paris.

Carton's trouble, says Stryver, is that he lacks energy and purpose. Stryver holds himself up as a shining example.

Carton merely laughs. He says it is gloomy talking about the past. He wants cheering up.

Stryver suggests they drink to Lucie's health, but this makes Carton even more morose.[2] He denies that Lucie is pretty or that he is interested in her.

He walks home through the chill dawn. The dusty, lifeless city reminds him of his own wasted life.

He flings himself on his bed and sleeps. There is nothing sadder than a man who has great feelings and abilities but cannot put them to good use.

1. chambers: lawyer's office.
2. morose: gloomy.

A Disturbing Tale

Dr. Manette's house.

There never was but one man worthy of her, and that was my brother Solomon.

Does the Doctor never refer to the shoe-making time?

Never.

Lucie and her father are living in a quiet house in Soho.[1] The Doctor seems much better and is practicing medicine again. Mr. Lorry often visits them.

Today Miss Pross answers the door, in a huffy mood. She claims Lucie is being pestered by hundreds of visitors. Miss Pross doesn't like any of them.

Mr. Lorry knows full well that Solomon is a heartless scoundrel who has spent every penny of Miss Pross's money. He changes the subject.

Touch that string[2] and he instantly changes for the worse.

Better leave it alone.

Workmen clearing an old dungeon found initials carved on a wall.

Though the Doctor never talks about the past, it haunts his mind. He sometimes paces his room at night as if still in his cell.

Actually, the "hundreds" of visitors are only two: Darnay chats pleasantly while Carton looks on. Miss Pross twitches with annoyance at the sight of them, and stomps off.

Darnay recounts a story he heard while in the Tower of London[3] awaiting trial.

My father— you are ill?

The workmen found letters that looked like DIC—a prisoner's initials? Or perhaps it was supposed to say DIG?

They dug into the floor and found a paper—a hidden message which could no longer be read.

For some reason this story alarms Dr. Manette. He springs up with a dazed and terrible look but quickly recovers. It has started to rain, and he says it was the raindrops that startled him.

1. Soho: a district of London which had many French residents at this time.
2. Touch that string: mention that subject.
3. Tower of London: a royal castle in London that was used as a prison for those accused of treason until the 20th century.

A French nobleman holds his fortnightly reception. He moves arrogantly through the visitors, bestowing a smile here and a wave of the hand there. People bow and fawn before him, for he is a great power at court and everyone wants to curry favor with him.[1]

One guest, the Marquis d'Evrémonde, receives neither smile nor wave from the great man. He sees he is in disfavor and curses beneath his breath. His handsome, cruel face is white with rage.

The Marquis drives away. His carriage tears through the narrow streets, sweeping heedlessly around corners. Women scream; men snatch children out of the way. But the Marquis is not concerned for the safety of ordinary people. Suddenly there is a sickening jolt.

The carriage has run over a child. A man is bending over the body, shrieking.

People gather round, horrified yet cowed and submissive. The Marquis looks at them as if they were rats come out of their holes.

The crowd parts and Defarge, the wine-seller, steps through. He comforts the dead child's father with words that are kindly but grim.

Contemptuously, the Marquis tosses him a coin. It is flung back at him by a bold-looking woman who is knitting. She glares at him as he drives off.

1. curry favor with him: flatter him, in an attempt to be liked by him.

DEATH IN THE NIGHT

The Marquis is returning to his country estate. His carriage thunders into the village near his château.[1] In its wretched main street there are signs of poverty everywhere. Women with misery-worn faces sit in doorways, shredding onions for their men's supper.

The Marquis calls to a road mender he had passed on the way. He demands to know why the roadmender has been staring at the carriage.

M.[3] Gabelle, the Marquis' bailiff,[4] forces the road mender to explain. He stutters out that he saw a man clinging to the underside of the coach. As it neared the village, the man dropped off and ran into the woods.

Cursing the road mender for not telling him at the time, the Marquis tells Gabelle to look into the matter, and drives on. As the coach passes a little burial ground, a woman calls out to him.

The Marquis thinks she wants food, but all she is seeking is some wood to mark her husband's grave. Like so many villagers, he lies under a bare mound of grass.

Without a word, the Marquis rides on. It is nightfall when he reaches the château, a magnificent, turreted house screened with trees. A servant with a torch comes out to meet him.

1. château: stately home, grand country house.
2. Monseigneur: my lord.
3. M.: short for "Monsieur," the French word for "Mr."
4. bailiff: the manager of the Marquis' estate—an unpopular man, because his duties include collecting the rent.
5. want: poverty, starvation.

> **What is that?**
>
> **Monseigneur, it is nothing.**

> **I know your diplomacy[1] would stop me and would know no scruple as to means.[2]**

In one of the smaller rooms, the Marquis dines at a table set for two. His guest is late. As the Marquis raises a glass to his lips, he thinks he sees a movement outside the window.

His guest is announced. It is his nephew, Charles Darnay. Darnay explains that he has been too busy to visit recently. He has to carry out a promise he made to his dying mother— and he knows his uncle will not approve of it.

> **If you were not in disgrace at court, a *lettre de cachet*[3] would have sent me to some fortress indefinitely.**
>
> **A new philosophy has become the mode. All very bad, very bad.**
>
> **Let us hope so.**
>
> **Detestation of the high is the involuntary homage of the low.[4]**

Darnay suspects his uncle of being behind the false charge of treason.

The Marquis misses the good old days when nobles could imprison whomever they wished.

Darnay retorts that the Evrémonde family has asserted its authority in such a way that its name has become the most detested in France.

> **It is a crumbling tower of waste, extortion,[5] oppression, nakedness, and suffering.**
>
> **Seeking it from me, you will forever seek it in vain, be assured.**

> Next morning…

Darnay's mother begged him to redress the wrong, but he has sought help everywhere in vain.

His uncle's attitude disgusts Darnay. He renounces his rights in the family title and property.

They part for the night, but the Marquis does not rise in the morning. He is found stone dead with a dagger through his heart. A paper attached to the hilt reads "Drive him fast to his tomb. This from JACQUES."

---

1. diplomacy: a polite word for "scheming."
2. would know no scruple as to means: would not care about being fair or unfair.
3. *lettre de cachet*: a letter with the King's seal, sentencing Darnay to prison without trial.
4. Detestation . . . of the low: Poor people cannot help showing their respect for the rich, if only by hating them.
5. extortion: getting money by threats.

THE WEDDING

Back in London.

Tell me when I ask you, not now. If Lucie should love you, tell me on your marriage morning.

Is it not a pity to lead no better life?

Darnay tells Dr. Manette of his secret hopes of marrying Lucie. He wants the Doctor to know his true identity, but Manette interrupts him abruptly.

Carton calls, with an air of purpose unusual for him. He finds Lucie alone. She exclaims that he looks unwell. That is his own fault, says Carton—the fault of the life he leads.

It is too late for that. I shall sink lower and lower.

You have been the last dream of my soul.

Think now and then that there is a man who would give his life to keep a life you love beside you.

Brokenly, Carton explains his feelings. Even if she had cared for him—an impossibility, he knows—he would only have brought her misery. He just wants to tell her she has stirred feelings in him that he thought were dead forever.

He wishes Lucie a happy married future and asks her to remember him as one who would do anything for her.

Meanwhile…

…in Defarge's wine shop.

Doomed to destruction—the château and all the race.

The road mender tells the pitiful story of the Marquis' killer. It was the grief-stricken father of the dead child, who had hidden beneath the coach. He has been publicly hanged.

The revolutionaries vow to see every member of the Marquis' family[1] exterminated.

Mme. Defarge keeps a terrible record. She knits the name of each victim into her memory, and as the list grows, so does her knitting.

1. every member of the Marquis' family: including, of course, his nephew Charles Darnay.

Good day, Jacques!

You mistake me for another. I am Ernest Defarge.

Miss Manette is going to marry the nephew of M. the Marquis.

They are both there for their merits. That is enough.

A stranger visits the wine shop. It is Barsad, now spying for the French government. He tries to trick the Defarges into giving themselves away.

The Defarges have been warned about Barsad. Mme. Defarge is knitting his name into her memory even now.

Defarge feels uneasy. Dr. Manette has suffered so much, it seems wrong to put his son-in-law on the record along with a wretch like Barsad.

London.

It is the day of Lucie's wedding. Lucie, Lorry, and Miss Pross are ready for church. Darnay and the Doctor have been having a private talk together. When they emerge, the Doctor is deathly pale.

Take her, Charles! She is yours!

After the ceremony the Doctor accompanies the couple to their carriage. He hands Lucie to Darnay with a smile. But as he turns back to the house, Lorry sees a great change in him, as if he had received a terrible blow.

Good God! What's that?

He is making shoes.

That night there is a sound of knocking from the Doctor's room.

For nine days the doctor's mind wanders. Lorry cares for him, and by the time Lucie returns he is his usual self. Sydney Carton congratulates the happy couple.

As the years pass, Carton becomes an old friend. When their daughter is born—a second Lucie—he is her favorite playmate.

THE PEOPLE RISE UP

July 1789: London.

That has a bad look.

Paris.

To me, women! We can kill as well as the men!

Six-year-old Lucie is already in bed when Mr. Lorry calls on the Darnays. Business at the bank is exhausting him. Wealthy Parisians are so alarmed by the political situation that they are rushing to transfer their money to England.

King Louis XVI tries to cope with demands for reform, but the starving citizens of Paris will not wait. They take to the streets, seizing any weapons they can find. Mme. Defarge heads a terrifying army of women.

The rioters attack the Bastille.

This huge prison has become a symbol of oppression. A white flag appears and the drawbridge is lowered. Defarge is at the head of the mob that surges over.

What is the meaning of 105 North Tower? Quick!

While rioters free the prisoners, Defarge has other business. He pins a prison guard against a wall.

There is no one there.

He is told it is the number of a cell. He forces the guard to take him there and light the walls with his torch.

Defarge rips apart the bed and the mattress, examining everything. Finally he gropes up the chimney—then, suddenly satisfied, he says they must go.

The revolution spreads to the countryside. Owners flee as peasants loot and burn their masters' property. The Marquis' mansion goes up in flames. Gabelle, the bailiff and rent collector, bars his door and spends the night in fear for his life.

After three years of revolutionary government, Tellson's French clients are fleeing in droves. Its Paris branch is in turmoil. Lorry is being sent there to sort things out. Darnay is worried; it is surely no job for an elderly man!

Darnay receives a desperate plea from France. M. Gabelle is to be tried for his life, accused of being an enemy of the people because he now serves Darnay, who is an emigrant.[1] Darnay feels honor-bound to help him.

Intending to return swiftly, he sets off for France. Once there, he is told that, as an aristocrat, he must travel under armed escort. He is forced to start at 3 A.M., linked by a rope to his guards.

When they reach the posting inn[4] at Beauvais, he finds an ominous crowd waiting for him to dismount. It is then that he learns that a new law has been passed, condemning all returning emigrants to death.

The guard who inspects his papers is Ernest Defarge, who asks whether he is the son-in-law of Dr. Manette. Darnay hopes he has found an ally.

He has been assigned to the prison of La Force. Darnay objects that he has come to help a fellow citizen. Is it not his right to be free to do so?

Darnay is placed in solitary confinement. Feeling as though he has been left for dead, he paces up and down the cold, damp cell.

1. serves Darnay, who is an emigrant: Darnay has inherited his murdered uncle's estate (though he did not want to), so he is now Gabelle's employer. Because Darnay has left the country, the revolutionaries are bound to regard him as a traitor.
2. supplicate: beg.
3. succor: help, rescue.
4. posting inn: an inn where long-distance travellers can hire fresh horses.

Freedom at Last?

Meanwhile…

Thank God that no one near and dear to me is in this dreadful town tonight.

What has brought you here?

Don't look, Lucie, my dear!

In his lodgings in Paris, Mr. Lorry listens to disturbing noises from the city.

Suddenly the door opens and Lucie rushes in, followed by Manette! They have come to protect Darnay. As a former Bastille prisoner, the Doctor is a hero to the revolutionaries, who have given them safe passage to Paris.

A noise from the courtyard draws Manette and Lucie to the window. Lorry stops them.

Make yourself known to the devils and get taken to La Force.

Help for the Bastille prisoner's kindred![1]

Save the prisoner Evrémonde at La Force!

Lorry ushers Lucie out, not wanting her to know that the noise outside is the sound of weapons being sharpened. He advises the Doctor to go to the revolutionaries and tell them who he is.

The revolutionaries have been dragging out prisoners and murdering them. But now Lorry sees Manette leaving the courtyard amidst cheers, with an escort of twenty revolutionaries, shoulder to shoulder, protecting him and hurrying him on.

Next day.

Is that his child?

Defarge brings a letter from Manette, and they set off for Lucie's lodgings. Mme. Defarge comes too—so that she can recognize Darnay's family.

Lucie is so overjoyed to hear that Darnay is safe that she kisses Mme. Defarge's hand.

With a cold stare, Mme. Defarge points her knitting needle at little Lucie. A sinister shadow seems to fall over the child and over the mother holding her.

1. kindred: relative.

Dr. Manette returns after four days. He cannot speak to Lucie of the horrors he has seen. He tells Lorry that in that time more than a thousand prisoners have been taken from their cells by the revolutionaries and slaughtered in the streets.

Manette has pleaded before the Revolutionary Tribunal[1] for Darnay's release. He thought he had succeeded, but at the last minute the decision was reversed, due to the influence of unnamed persons.

Lucie and her father will not leave Paris until Darnay is free. The Doctor is appointed physician to the prisons. This allows him to obtain news of Darnay from La Force.

He tells Lucie that if she stands in a certain spot Darnay can see her from his cell window, though she cannot see him.

For more than a year, in all weathers, she stands in this spot daily. Mme. Defarge sometimes passes and glares at her, but does not speak.

January 21, 1793.

Nothing can happen to him without my knowledge. I know that I can save him.

France has become a republic, and now Louis XVI is executed. The mood of the time is not hopeful for Darnay.

Throughout the Reign of Terror[2] Manette remains in favor with the revolutionary authorities and works unharmed. He tells Lucie not to fear for Darnay's safety.

Darnay is tried at last. Manette testifies that Darnay has been tried for his life as a foe of England and friend of America.[3] Darnay is carried home in triumph.

1. Revolutionary Tribunal: the court set up by the revolutionaries to try their enemies.
2. Reign of Terror: the period from September 1793 to July 1794 when thousands were executed by the revolutionaries.
3. friend of America: the French revolutionaries regarded the American revolutionaries as brothers.

A KNOCK AT THE DOOR

Though Darnay is now free, he has no permit to leave France, so escape is impossible. On the afternoon of his release, he is sitting with Lucie and the Doctor, making plans, when there is a sudden knock at the door.

Four rough men armed with sabers and pistols enter the room.

The men have come to re-arrest Darnay. He must appear before the Tribunal again tomorrow, when he will learn the reason for his re-arrest.

The Doctor stands as if turned to stone with astonishment. He asks the men's leader if he is aware who he is.

Darnay has been denounced to the Revolutionary Committee. As a true patriot, says the man, the Doctor must not stand against the will of the people.

The Doctor insists on knowing the names of his son-in-law's accusers. At first the man is unwilling to reply. When he does give an answer, it is a puzzling one.

The man will not say who this "other" is. He says that all will be made clear tomorrow. Darnay is escorted away to the Conciergerie.[2]

1. Citizen: the title used by the revolutionaries to address everyone. They objected to old titles such as "monsieur" and "monseigneur," which suggested that some people were better than others.
2. the Conciergerie: another of Paris's medieval prisons, still standing today.

26

Meanwhile…

OH!

Don't call me Solomon. Do you want to be the death of me?

Unaware of what has happened, Miss Pross, escorted by Jerry Cruncher, is shopping for the Manettes. While they are waiting to be served, she suddenly gives a scream and claps her hands with joy. She has recognized one of the customers!

It is her brother Solomon, the scoundrel in whom she has such touching faith. She is amazed and overjoyed, and makes a great fuss over him. But for some reason he is far from pleased to be recognized.

You was a spy at the Bailey![1] What was you called at the time?

Barsad.

I present myself here to beg a little talk with your brother.

Solomon hustles them out of the shop. Jerry is sure he's seen him before—but at that time his name certainly wasn't Pross.

A voice from behind startles them. It is Carton, newly arrived in Paris in the hope of being of service to Lucie. He has been following Barsad for a purpose.

Under threat?

Oh! Did I say that?

Carton tells Barsad he knows he is a spy. He has a proposal to put to him that is best not discussed in public. He suggests, as casually as possible, that Barsad had better accompany him to Tellson's Bank.

Carton manages to suggest that he could make things very uncomfortable for him if he doesn't. Reluctantly, Barsad agrees to go with him. He tells his sister that if any trouble comes of this, it's her fault.

1. the Bailey: the Old Bailey (see page 12).

A Hand of Cards

I left him safe and free within these two hours!

Mr. Lorry's rooms at Tellson's Bank.

When matters are desperate, desperate games must be played for desperate stakes.

Lorry greets Barsad coldly, remembering him from the trial. Carton tells Lorry the alarming news that he has just heard: Darnay has been taken to the Conciergerie.

Carton fears the worst. The fact that Dr. Manette has not been able to prevent the arrest suggests that powerful forces are bent on Darnay's destruction. But why?

The friend I propose to win, is Mr. Barsad.

You need have good cards, sir.

I'll run them over. I'll see what I have.

In these times, no man's life is safe. Everything is a gamble—and the stakes are high. What they need now is a friend at the Conciergerie.

Carton calls for brandy, drains his glass, and begins to examine an imaginary hand of cards.

Mr. Barsad, now working for the French government, formerly worked for the English government, the enemy of France and freedom.

That's an excellent card—

Mr. Barsad, now turnkey,[1] now prisoner, always spy, represents himself to his employers under an assumed name.

That's a very good card.

—as good as proof, in these suspicious times, that Mr. Barsad is that English traitor in the bosom of the Republic whom everyone speaks of and no one can find.

28   1. turnkey: jailer.

Have you followed my hand, Mr. Barsad?

Not to understand your play.

I play my ace: denunciation of Mr. Barsad to the nearest Section Committee.[1] Look over your hand, Mr. Barsad, and see what you have.

You scarcely seem to like your hand. Do you play?

You told me you had a proposal. What is it?

I tell you once and for all that there is no such thing as an escape possible.

Why need you tell me what I have not asked?

Carton asks whether Barsad has access to the keys of the Conciergerie. The spy assumes he is hoping to help the prisoner escape.

Carton slowly pours the last of his brandy out upon the hearth, as if to mark some grave decision.

Then he draws Barsad aside. Whatever the proposal may be, it is to remain a secret between the two of them.

1. Section Committee: local government organization. Paris was divided into 48 "sections," each with its own committee. They had a reputation for being ruthless.

THE TRIBUNAL

But access will not save him.

I never said it would.

Anxious and unhappy, but very beautiful.

Ah!

I hoped to have left her in perfect safety.

When Barsad has gone, Lorry inquires doubtfully what Carton has achieved. Carton replies that Barsad is getting him access to the prisoner.

Carton begs Lorry not to mention his arrangement with Barsad to Lucie. It might worry her. Better not to say that Carton is in Paris. He asks how Lucie is looking.

Lorry's work in Paris is now over. He has a permit to leave, but he fears for Lucie.

But you are young.

I am not old, but my young way was never the way to age. Enough of me.

You will be careful? You know the consequences of mixing them?

Perfectly.

Lucie loves Lorry for his caring concern; his is a life well spent, says Carton feelingly. How good it must be to know that one's life has served a purpose!

Carton bids Lorry goodnight. Outside, he stops beneath a lamp to write on a scrap of paper.

Knowing Paris well from his student days, he makes his way through dark and winding streets to a dingy little pharmacy, where he hands over the paper.

I am the resurrection and the life, saith the Lord:

he that believeth in me, though he were dead, yet shall he live;

and whoever liveth and believeth in me, shall never die.

Carton takes the packets the pharmacist has made up and steps into the night. He cannot sleep; his heart is too full. As he wanders the quiet city, words from the Burial Service[1] arise in his mind and return to him constantly:

1. Burial Service: the prayers said when a dead person is buried.

Darnay is brought before the Tribunal.

Five judges and a savage-looking jury sit in judgement. Lucie, Lorry, and Manette are in agonized suspense. Hidden from them at the back, Carton looks on. The Public Prosecutor reads the charge.

"Charles Evrémonde, called Darnay, is a denounced enemy of the Republic, one of a family of tyrants proscribed[1] for having used their privileges for the infamous oppression of the people."

"First: Ernest Defarge, wine vendor of St. Antoine."

The President asks to hear the names of the accusers. He is told there are three, all present in court. Their names are read out one by one.

"Second: his wife, Thérèse Defarge."

"Third: Alexandre Manette, physician."

At the third name the court erupts in uproar. Dr. Manette sits as if turned to stone. Pale and trembling, he protests that this is surely a mistake, a forgery.

Defarge takes the witness stand. He testifies that, on the day the Bastille was taken, he examined the cell where Dr. Manette had been imprisoned and found a paper hidden behind a stone in the chimney. There is absolute silence in the court.

Let the paper be read.

1. proscribed: condemned.

THE TESTIMONY[1]

"I, Alexandre Manette, write this in my cell in the year 1767. On a night in December 1757, I was walking near the Seine[2] when a carriage stopped and two men wrapped in cloaks got out.

"They were armed, I was not. I was forcibly driven to a lonely country house where a young woman lay in a frenzy of delirium, her arms bound to her sides. She maintained a constant shrieking of the same words: "My husband, my father, my brother!"

"While I was doing what I could for the woman, one of the men—they were brothers—said there was another patient.

"He showed me a boy lying in a loft, with a deep wound in his chest. With savage contempt, the man said this peasant had dared to cross swords with the man's brother, an aristocrat.

"The dying boy told me his story. The common people's sense of injustice burst from him like fire.

"The woman was his sister. The younger of the two noblemen had demanded the use of her. To make her yield, they harnessed her sick husband to a cart. He was forced to pull it until he died.

"Though she was expecting her husband's child, the brothers seized the helpless widow. The boy saw her carried off. When he told his father, the blow killed him. The boy sent his other, younger sister away, where these men would never find her.

1. Testimony: a sworn statement given by a witness.
2. Seine: the river that flows through Paris.
3. serf: a peasant who did not have the freedom to leave his master's land. Serfdom was abolished in France in 1789.

"I summon you, to the last of your bad race, to answer for these things.

"The boy had found a sword and sought revenge. With his last breath he cursed them.

"Despite my care, his sister also died. The brothers now regarded me with open hatred, knowing I was aware that their horrific actions had caused these deaths. I left, refusing payment.

"Soon after this, I was visited by a stranger who gave her name as the Marquise d'Evrémonde. She had learned of her husband's cruelty and wanted to make amends.

I want to help the poor girl's sister, if I can.

It is for thine own dear sake. Thou wilt be faithful, little Charles?

"I regretted I could not help, for I had no idea where the boy's surviving sister might be. The Marquise insisted she must find out, for her baby son's[1] sake. She felt he could never prosper till this wrong was righted.

"I was so troubled that I wrote a letter to the Minister, reporting the deaths. That night I was at home with my beloved English wife when an unknown caller summoned me to an urgent case.

I denounce them, and their descendants, to the last of their race.

"Once outside my door, I was seized and gagged. The Marquis appeared from the shadows with my letter, which he burned before my eyes. Not a word was spoken. I was brought here, to this prison which is now my living grave.

"These Evrémondes, lacking even the grace to tell me whether my beloved wife is alive or dead, are truly lost to God.[2] In my unbearable agony, I curse their family to the utmost and forever."

1. her baby son: Charles Darnay.
2. lost to God: so evil that God would forbid them forgiveness and salvation.

AFTER THE VERDICT

After such a denunciation, nothing can save Darnay. There is a roar as each juror announces his vote: GUILTY—to the guillotine within twenty-four hours!

Lucie is allowed to say a last, agonizing farewell to her husband. She is brought home unconscious by Carton, who urges her stricken father to make one last plea to the authorities for mercy.

Carton tells Lorry he suggested this purely for Lucie's sake. He does not want her to reproach herself in the future by thinking that they had not tried.

Leaving Lucie in the care of Miss Pross, Carton now sets off purposefully for the district of St. Antoine.

He enters Defarge's wine shop and asks for wine—not in his usual excellent French, but with a heavy English accent.

Carton makes himself as noticeable as possible by drinking a health to the Republic. Then he pretends to be puzzling over a French newspaper. The customers give him him curious glances.

Mme. Defarge talks gleefully about the coming execution. She is now building up a case against Lucie.

Why is she so implacable?[1] Because the raving woman in the Doctor's account was her sister; the dead boy, her brother!

1. implacable: unable or unwilling to let anything satisfy her desire.

"I cannot find it and I must have it. Where is my bench?"

"Give me my work! What is to become of us if those shoes are not done tonight?"

Once he is sure the revolutionaries have noticed the Englishman who looks like Darnay, Carton returns to Lorry's rooms. They are expecting the Doctor, and as the hours pass they grow increasingly anxious. At midnight he appears. One glance tells them the worst: his mind has wandered—he is the old shoemaker again.

It is hopeless to reason with him. They put him in a chair by the fire. He stares vacantly and does not know them.

"Don't ask me why. I have a reason—a good one."

"Thank God!"

"Have your horses in starting trim[1] at two o'clock in the afternoon."

Carton begs Lorry, in this hour of crisis, to listen to his instructions and promise to obey them exactly.

Carton picks up the Doctor's coat and a paper falls out. It is a permit for the Doctor, his daughter, and her child to leave France.

Manette and Lucie must leave with Lorry tomorrow, Carton insists. Mme. Defarge plans to denounce the Manettes and get their permit cancelled.

"Why not?"

"I don't know. I prefer not to."

Carton hands his own exit permit to Lorry, saying that he is going to see Darnay tomorrow at the Conciergerie and had better not take it into the prison with him.

Carton and Lorry help the stricken doctor home. Carton impresses on Lorry that they must all be in the coach at two tomorrow, and the instant he joins them from the Conciergerie they must set off for England.

1. in starting trim: harnessed and ready to leave.

IN THE CONCIERGERIE

Darnay is writing farewells. He tells Lucie he knew nothing of his family's part in her father's suffering. He tells the Doctor not to blame himself, and he thanks Lorry. He forgets Carton—his mind is full of the others.

Day dawns: the last day of his life. The execution is at three o'clock. He notes each hour as the clock strikes. Noon passes, and one o'clock. There is suddenly a rattle of keys in the door; it is flung open and Carton enters the cell.

Carton insists, with terrible urgency, that there is no time for questions. He must just obey. Darnay is bewildered by his manner.

With a strength of will that seems supernatural, Carton forces Darnay to change coats and cravats with him.

Carton next insists on dictating a letter. As Darnay bends to write, he notices a vaporous smell and glimpses Carton moving up behind him.

Realizing what Carton means to do, he tries to rise. It is too late. His limbs feel heavy. A hand closes over his nostrils.

Carton orders his accomplice, Barsad, to get the unconscious man to Lorry's coach immediately.

Alone in the cell, Carton adjusts his clothes and hair. He listens tensely for any sound of an alarm being raised, but hears nothing. Soon the clock strikes two.

Three o'clock approaches. Carton hears the clang of cell doors being unlocked. His own is flung open by a jailer who carries a list in his hand.

Carton is taken to a dark room filled with silent people, mostly staring at the ground. He tries to avoid being noticed.

A timid, pale-faced young woman comes over to him. She reminds him that she is the seamstress[1] he met when they were both prisoners in La Force.

Like him, she has been accused on no evidence at all. She begs him to let her sit beside him in the tumbril[2] on the way to the guillotine and hold his hand.

As the young woman gazes into his face, she realizes she is not speaking to Evrémonde. This is a different man!

At one of the gates out of Paris, a coach with four passengers attempting to leave the city is stopped by the military guard.

Mr. Lorry hands the guard the papers. As the guard reads out the names, Lorry identifies each occupant in turn.

The guard glances briefly at the Englishman slumped in a corner, who seems to have fainted.

The papers are in order; the coach may go. Not daring to drive fast for fear of being noticed, its passengers clasp each other in mingled terror and joy.

1. seamstress: woman who earns her living by sewing.
2. tumbril: a farm cart, used to transport prisoners to execution.
3. advocate: lawyer.
4. swoon: faint.

THREE O'CLOCK

The working people of Paris are especially gleeful today—Evrémonde goes to the guillotine! But for Mme. Defarge that is not enough.

She means to catch Lucie in the act of mourning an enemy of the Republic—a capital crime.[1] She will be back in time for the execution.

With a look of terrible purpose, Mme. Defarge sets off for the Manettes' lodgings. Like a true patriot, she carries a loaded pistol.

The Manettes have just left in the coach. Miss Pross is waiting for Jerry to bring up another vehicle for them to follow in. She is startled to see Mme. Defarge.

Miss Pross shuts the doors to hide the fact that the occupants have fled. She bars the way to Lucie's room.

Mme. Defarge demands to be let through. Miss Pross is equally determined not to let her discover that Lucie's room is empty.

Neither understands the other's language, but their meaning is clear. Mme. Defarge hurls herself at Miss Pross, who grasps at her in defense.

Mme. Defarge reaches for her weapon; Miss Pross sees the pistol and strikes at it. There is a flash and a terrific noise.

When the smoke clears there is only stillness. The entire world is silent; poor Miss Pross has gone totally deaf. She steps over the body and goes in search of Jerry.

1. a capital crime: one for which the penalty is death.

Six tumbrils carry today's victims to the guillotine. Each afternoon people line the streets to watch the carts go by. For them the executions are an entertainment. Along the route, the people are continually calling to the mounted guards with the same question: which one is Evrémonde?

The guards point to a man in the third cart. He pays no heed at all to the crowd, but is talking to a frail young woman as if they were alone together.

Around the scaffold,[1] bloodthirsty women take their customary seats. But there is one empty chair with knitting on it.

Carton helps the young woman from the cart, turning her back to the scaffold so she cannot see the blade descending.

The seamstress fears years of loneliness before her living family joins her in the life after death. Carton reassures her. Then her name is called and she is gone.

Carton mounts the scaffold, thinking not of himself but of Lucie's future happiness, her father recovered and her husband by her side. He imagines them with a son named Sydney—a precious name, honored by them all.

1. scaffold: raised platform on which executions are carried out.

The end

CHARLES DICKENS (1812–1870)

harles Dickens was easily the most popular novelist writing in English in the 19th century—and most people would agree that he was the greatest.

He was born in 1812 to moderately well-off parents (his father was a naval clerk), but the family's lifestyle changed when his foolishly extravagant father was arrested for debt and sent to the Marshalsea, a notorious debtors' prison. While Charles's mother and the younger children joined his father in the prison, Charles, who was only 12, was sent to live alone in a lodging house in North London. There he worked 12 hours a day in a boot-blacking factory to earn the family some money. He never forgot this experience. It taught him about the dreadful conditions in which poor people lived and worked. Later, as a successful novelist, he used his writing to expose such injustices.

Charles Dickens, photographed by Herbert Watkins in 1858.

BECOMING A WRITER

The family's fortunes improved enough for Charles to return briefly to school, but at 15 he had to start work as a clerk in a solicitor's office. He escaped from this boring job by teaching himself shorthand and becoming a journalist. He was a quick and lively reporter with a great relish for oddities of character. Soon he was writing humorous articles based on his observations of London life. A collection of these, published in 1836 as *Sketches by Boz*, was such a success that he was immediately invited to write another book. This was *The Pickwick Papers*, which appeared in 1837 and was a runaway success.

SERIALS

From this moment Dickens never looked back. As soon as one book appeared, his readers were impatiently waiting for the next. He was constantly at work, often starting on a new book while he was still writing installments of the previous one. All his major novels first came out as serials in magazines. This meant that people who couldn't afford the price of an expensive three-volume novel could still buy his work. This was important to Dickens, who loved to feel that he was in touch with a wide public and could stir their consciences through his writing.

A BUSY LIFE

Dickens had enormous energy. As well as completing 14 full-length novels and countless shorter pieces, he was also a journalist, magazine editor, lecturer, travel writer, playwright, and amateur actor. He used his acting skill to great effect in giving public readings from his novels, mesmerizing audiences by his ability to conjure up vivid characters. He took these performances on tour in England and the United States. One particularly gruelling series of 76 readings, which he gave in America in the winter of 1867–1868, finally broke his health and he died two years later, at age 59. He was at work on his unfinished novel *The Mystery of Edwin Drood* on the day before he died.

DICKENS THE SOCIAL CRITIC

In his novels Dickens was a fierce critic of the poverty and inequality he saw all around him in Victorian society. He campaigned for parliamentary reform, better schooling, better housing and sanitation, and for the abolition of slavery. His greatest asset in getting people to think seriously about these things was his ability to entertain. His novels are all good stories, packed with characters whose quirks and oddities can be sinister, endearing, or hilarious, and who all have that larger-than-life quality that we still call "Dickensian."

BOOKS BY CHARLES DICKENS

1836: *Sketches by Boz*
1837: *The Pickwick Papers*
1838: *Oliver Twist*
1839: *Nicholas Nickleby*
1841: *The Old Curiosity Shop*
1841: *Barnaby Rudge*
1843: *A Christmas Carol*
1844: *Martin Chuzzlewit*
1845: *The Cricket on the Hearth*
1848: *Dombey and Son*

1850: *David Copperfield*
1853: *Bleak House*
1854: *Hard Times*
1857: *Little Dorrit*
1859: *A Tale of Two Cities*
1861: *Great Expectations*
1865: *Our Mutual Friend*
1870: *The Mystery of Edwin Drood* (unfinished at the time of Dickens's death).

Dickens saw his novels as weapons in the fight against social injustice. For this reason, he normally wrote about his own times. *A Tale of Two Cities* is one of only two novels by him that have a historical setting (the other is *Barnaby Rudge*). Both these tales are set in times of great social unrest when overpowering grievances led people to take the law into their own hands.

Dickens's description of the savage Paris mob and its unrelenting hatred—typified by Mme. Defarge—shows his horror at its inhumanity. At the same time he is at great pains to point out that this inhumanity is not a characteristic of the French people; it is the result of injustice and oppression, and the same thing will happen in any people subject to tyranny. This is how he puts it in *A Tale of Two Cities*:

Crush humanity out of shape once more, under similar hammers, and it will twist itself into the same tortured forms. Sow the same seed of rapacious licence and oppression over again, and it will surely yield the same fruit according to its kind.

This was a message for Dickens's own time and his own country. People in 19th-century Britain saw poverty worsening around them. They feared that the French Revolution, which happened only 70 years before Dickens was writing, would be repeated in England. Dickens's message to them is: "Do something about it!"

SYDNEY CARTON'S SACRIFICE

Though the political message of the book is contained in stunning descriptions of the street scenes of Paris and London, it is above all the romantic storyline which has made *A Tale of Two Cities* one of Dickens's best-loved novels. Dickens said he got the central idea for the plot while he was acting in an amateur production of a play by his friend Wilkie Collins, *The Frozen Deep*. Dickens played the part of its flawed but noble hero, who sacrifices his life so that his friend can survive to be with the woman they both love. Dickens said that this idea completely took possession of him while he was writing the book, so much so that he felt he was himself experiencing all the love and suffering he described. Dickens's own emotional life was in turmoil at this time. He was separating from his wife and in love with another, much younger woman, and this may explain his highly charged response to Collins's hero.

SUCCESS ON STAGE AND SCREEN

A Tale of Two Cities appeared in 1859. Like all of Dickens's novels, it was first published as a serial, this time in a new journal Dickens had just launched, called *All the Year Round*. This was a weekly publication, not a monthly one as previously, so Dickens had to write under even more pressure than usual, to meet a deadline every week. He always wrote his books in installments, keeping just ahead of his readers.

The book was a big success and Dickens was pleased with it, describing it at the time as "the best story I have

A still from the 1935 film of A Tale of Two Cities.

written." Its exciting twists of plot, its love triangle, and its final sacrifice make it ideal for the stage. The role of Sydney Carton, the talented wastrel with the heart of gold, had an immediate appeal for actors and audiences. Even in the book, he totally eclipses the boring hero Darnay. On stage or on the screen, his words of sublime self-sacrifice on the scaffold have given a host of actors their moment of glory.

Dickens realized this himself. Even before the last installment was out, he was sending proofs to a friend in Paris to see if he thought it would be a success on the French stage. It wasn't put on in France, but there was a stage version, supervised by Dickens, at the Lyceum, London, in 1860. The most famous stage adaptation was an 1899 version called *The Only Way*, in which

the great romantic actor John Martin Harvey had a huge success as Carton. The production was revived many times; Martin Harvey claimed that by the time he retired he had played the role 3,000 times. He repeated it in a silent film version in 1925. The first sound version, in 1935, starred Ronald Colman as Carton, and Dirk Bogarde played the role in 1958. There have been many TV serializations. Musical versions were staged in Florida in 2007, and by an all-female opera company in Japan in 1984 and 2003.

A spin-off novel by Susan Alleyn called *A Far Better Rest*, retelling the story from Carton's point of view, appeared in 2000. Diane Mayer's 2005 novel, *Evrémonde*, imagines what happened to Darnay and Lucie after the Revolution.

REVOLUTIONARY ANSWERS

The French Revolution of 1789 was still quite recent history when Dickens was writing, and he assumed that his readers would know about it. Today's readers might like a few questions answered:

Why did Darnay's approval of America suggest that he was a French spy?
Because France supported America in its fight for independence from Britain.

What were lettres de cachet?
They were written orders from the king, authorizing immediate actions that could not be repealed. Wealthy people were able to buy orders for imprisonment without trial and use them against their opponents.

Why did French people want to overthrow King Louis XVI?
Very few did at first. They rebelled because they wanted him to do something about the glaring injustices in the way the country was run. The nobles and clergy were rich and privileged but paid no taxes. The other 96% of the population—mostly very poor peasants—paid all the taxes and had few rights. French kings ruled absolutely; they could make decisions without consulting anyone. Many people felt that this system was wrong. They wanted royal power to be limited by a Constitution, as it was in England, and they forced Louis XVI to agree to this.

Why was Louis tried as a traitor?
Although Louis seemed to accept the Constitution, people suspected, with good reason, that he was secretly encouraging other European powers to intervene and bring back absolute monarchy. Since the Constitution was now the law of the land, scheming to get rid of it amounted to treason. Hard-line revolutionaries declared France a Republic and put the king on trial. He was charged with bankrupting the nation, plotting against the Revolution, trying to flee, accepting a Constitution he was plotting to destroy, and helping foreign powers to invade.

What was the Reign of Terror?
The period from September 1793 to July 1794 when panic over fears of invasion led to thousands of suspected anti-revolutionaries being sent to the guillotine. A Committee of Public Safety was set up to defend the Revolution. It was controlled by the most radical revolutionaries, known as Jacobins, and its discussions were secret.

What was the Revolutionary Tribunal?
This was a criminal court set up by the Committee of Public Safety to deal with anyone suspected of working against the Revolution. People were denounced to the Tribunal on the merest suspicion. They could not call witnesses in their defense, and the penalty was always death. In two years the Tribunal sent over 2,700 people to the guillotine.

What was the Bastille?
It was a fortress, built in the late 14th century and later used as a prison and as a weapon store. By the time it was stormed by the revolutionaries on July 14, 1789, there were only seven prisoners left. Over the next few months the building was almost entirely demolished.

What was the Conciergerie?
A royal palace, built in the early 14th century and used as a prison since 1391. During the Revolution it held prisoners due to appear before the Revolutionary Tribunal, and those awaiting execution. The Tribunal sat in the Great Hall of the Conciergerie. Unlike the Bastille, the Conciergerie is still standing and is now open to the public.

Why were returning emigrants executed?
Many aristocrats who had fled abroad tried to raise foreign help to quell the Revolution. As a result, any who were unwise enough to return to France were automatically treated as traitors.

Who was Jacques?
Jacques had been a traditional name for a peasant. Dickens may also have been thinking of the 14th-century rebellion of French peasants against oppressive nobles which was known as the Jacquerie. Defarge and his companions use the name as a coded way of showing that they are revolutionaries.

What was St. Antoine?
Since medieval times, St. Antoine had been the district of Paris where craftsmen lived and worked. Louis XVI himself encouraged the setting up of factories and workshops there. It was a poor area that became a breeding ground for working-class revolutionaries. The notorious Bastille prison was nearby.

Why did they use the guillotine?
The guillotine was a tall frame with a very heavy, razor-sharp blade that fell with speed and precision. It was designed to provide a merciful death, compared to a sword or an axe, which could take several blows to sever the neck. The Revolutionary government decided in 1791 that it would be fair for all citizens to face the same death penalty; previously, commoners had been hanged. A committee was set up to look into the most painless method. Dr. Joseph-Ignace Guillotin, a professor of anatomy, was on the committee and, though he did not design the machine (it may have been in use in England as early as the 13th century), his name has stuck. The guillotine continued in use in France until the abolition of the death penalty in 1981.

Sydney Carton on the scaffold; a painting by Frederick Barnard, 1882.

Although *A Tale of Two Cities* is a work of fiction, it is based on the real events of the French Revolution. Dickens worked out the timescale of his novel very carefully. This is how the fictional events fit in with the real-life ones:

FACT

1756 Louis XV's grandson, the future Louis XVI, marries Austrian archduchess Marie-Antoinette.

1774 Louis XVI comes to the throne. He is well-meaning but weak, and lacks political ability.

1775 American Revolutionary War begins between Britain and her colonies. France gives America covert support at first, and later sends forces. American ideals of freedom and equality influence French political thinkers. Jean Jacques Rousseau writes: "Man is born free. No man has any natural authority over others; force does not give anyone that right. The power to make laws belongs to the people and only to the people."

1776 American Declaration of Independence.

1787–1789 Three years of bad harvests in France cause food prices to soar. Peasants starve while the nobility, clergy, and court live in luxury.

May 1789 The government is hugely in debt, due to the cost of foreign wars. Louis XVI calls a meeting of the Estates General (French parliament), which cannot agree on what to do.

June 20, 1789 The self-styled National Assembly swears the Tennis Court Oath, named after the indoor court in which it meets. It vows not to disband until the king agrees to a new constitution.

July 14, 1789 A rioting Paris mob attacks the Bastille prison and kills its governor. In the country, peasants attack châteaus, burn property and title deeds, and murder owners. Aristocrats begin to flee abroad.

FICTION

1757 Dr. Manette is forced by two aristocratic brothers to attend a delirious young woman and her dying brother. To prevent Manette revealing their cruelty, the brothers use their aristocratic privileges to imprison him without trial.

1757–1775 Manette is held in solitary confinement in the Bastille, where he occupies himself by learning to make shoes.

1767 After ten years of imprisonment, Manette writes an impassioned denunciation of the brothers and every member of their family. He hides it in the chimney of his cell.

1775 Manette, now in a state of mental confusion, is released into the care of his former servant, Ernest Defarge, and brought to England by his daughter Lucie and banker Jarvis Lorry. Lucie's devotion restores his sanity. By chance, Charles Darnay travels to England on the same boat. His frequent journeys between France and England give rise to the suspicion that he is a French spy.

1780 Darnay is tried for treason in England. Sydney Carton helps to defend him. Despite the evidence of the spy Barsad, Darnay is acquitted.

1780–1789 Darnay visits his uncle, the Marquis d'Evrémonde, who is murdered that night by a victim of his cruelty.
   Barsad, now spying for the French government, visits the Defarges' wine shop. The revolutionaries are making a secret record of people they intend to see executed.
   Back in England, Darnay marries Lucie Manette, and their daughter Lucie is born. Carton and Lorry become friends of the family.

July 1789 Lorry tells the Manettes that the Paris branch of his bank is overwhelmed with business, through aristocrats trying to get their money out of France.
   During the storming of the Bastille, Defarge finds Manette's letter denouncing the Evrémonde family.
   The Marquis' château is burned down.

FACT

August 1789 The National Assembly issues the Declaration of the Rights of Man, modelled on the United States's Declaration of Independence. The king is forced to accept it but has no intention of supporting it.

October 1789 A Paris mob captures Louis XVI and his family as they try to escape, and places them under house arrest in Paris. Meanwhile, he and the queen are secretly encouraging foreign rulers to invade and restore absolute monarchy.

June 1791 Louis and his family attempt to escape to the Austrian Netherlands, hoping to return at the head of an army. Louis is recognized and brought back to Paris.

September 1791 A new constitution is finally proclaimed, making the monarch little more than a figurehead. Louis is forced to sign an oath of loyalty to it.

1792 The September Massacres. Fearing an invasion, France has declared war on Austria and Prussia. Rumors that the Prussians are marching on Paris cause panic. The Paris mob slaughters thousands of prison inmates, on the grounds that they are anti-revolutionaries who would support the enemy.

September 21, 1792 The monarchy is abolished and a republic declared.

December 1792 Trial of Louis XVI.

January 21, 1793 Execution of Louis XVI.

September 1793–July 1794 The Reign of Terror. Thousands of suspected anti-revolutionaries are sent to the guillotine.

1795–1799 The Directory. The Jacobins (hardline revolutionaries) lose their grip on power and moderates take over. A new government, the Directory, is established, with five directors to run the country. It is soon in crisis through military setbacks, lack of money, and food shortages.

1799 Napoleon Bonaparte seizes power. A new constitution makes him First Consul of France.

December 2, 1804 Napoleon crowns himself Emperor of France.

FICTION

1789–1792 Throughout this troubled time, the Darnays and Dr. Manette live peacefully in a quiet part of London. Carton and Lorry are regular visitors.

1792 Lorry is sent to his bank's Paris branch to prevent records being destroyed in the disorder engulfing the city. He takes Jerry Cruncher with him for protection.

Darnay receives a letter from his agent Gabelle, begging him to bear witness at his trial and save his life. He leaves for France, where he is arrested as an emigrant, taken to Paris, and imprisoned in La Force.

Dr. Manette and Lucie rush to Paris, hoping to use the Doctor's status as an ex-Bastille prisoner to get Darnay released. Miss Pross, Jerry Cruncher, and little Lucie accompany them.

1792–1794 Manette saves Darnay from execution but his imprisonment continues.

1794 Sydney Carton comes to Paris hoping to help Lucie.

Darnay is at last brought before the Revolutionary Tribunal and Dr. Manette obtains his release. He is re-arrested the same day, due to the Defarges' denunciation and Dr. Manette's written account, retried the following day, and sentenced to the guillotine.

Carton recognizes Barsad and blackmails him into providing access to Darnay in prison.

Carton is executed in Darnay's place.

INDEX

IF YOU LIKED THIS BOOK, YOU MIGHT LIKE TO TRY THESE OTHER TITLES IN BARRON'S *GRAPHIC CLASSICS* SERIES:

Adventures of Huckleberry Finn Mark Twain
Dracula Bram Stoker
Dr. Jekyll and Mr. Hyde Robert Louis Stevenson
Frankenstein Mary Shelley
The Hunchback of Notre Dame Victor Hugo
Journey to the Center of the Earth Jules Verne

Kidnapped Robert Louis Stevenson
Macbeth William Shakespeare
The Man in the Iron Mask Alexandre Dumas
Moby Dick Herman Melville
Oliver Twist Charles Dickens
The Three Musketeers Alexandre Dumas
Treasure Island Robert Louis Stevenson

FOR MORE INFORMATION ON CHARLES DICKENS:

The Dickens Page
www.lang.nagoya-u.ac.jp/~matsuoka/Dickens.html

Charles Dickens
www.helsinki.fi/kasv/nokol/dickens.html